C. Schatz

Are You My Mother?

leonie

Written and Illustrated by
P. D. EASTMAN

COLLINS AND HARVILL

To My Mother

Trademark of Random House, Inc., William Collins Sons & Co. Ltd., Authorised User

ISBN 0 00 171108 3
© 1960 BY P. D. EASTMAN
A BEGINNER BOOK PUBLISHED BY ARRANGEMENT WITH
RANDOM HOUSE, INC., NEW YORK, NEW YORK
FIRST PUBLISHED IN GREAT BRITAIN 1962
PRINTED IN GREAT BRITAIN
COLLINS CLEAR-TYPE PRESS: LONDON AND GLASGOW

A mother bird sat on
her egg.

The egg jumped.

"Oh oh!" said the
mother bird. "My baby
will be here! He will
want to eat."

"I must get something for my baby bird to eat!" she said. "I will be back!"

So away she went.

The egg jumped. It
jumped, and jumped, and
jumped!

Out came the baby
bird!

"Where is my mother?"
he said.

He looked for her.

He looked up. He did
not see her.

He looked down. He did
not see her.

"I will go and look for
her," he said.

So away he went.

Down, out of the tree
he went.

Down, down, down! It
was a long way down.

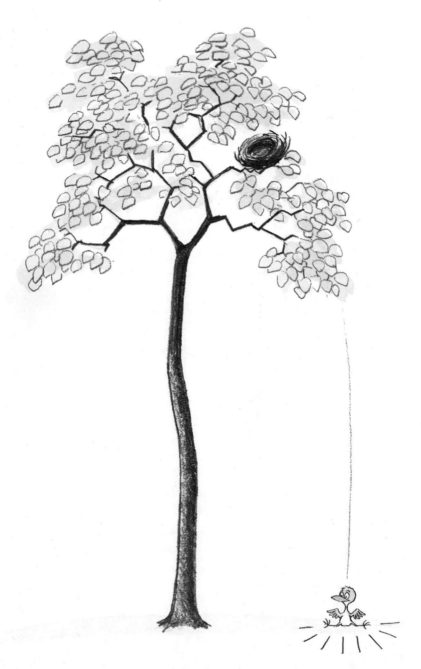

The baby bird could
not fly.

He could not fly, but
he could walk. "Now I
will go and find my
mother," he said.

He did not know what
his mother looked like. He
went right by her. He did
not see her.

He came to a kitten.
"Are you my mother?"
he said to the kitten.

The kitten just looked
and looked. It did not
say a thing.

The kitten was not his
mother, so he went on.

Then he came to a
hen.

"Are you my mother?"
he said to the hen.

"No," said the hen.

The kitten was not
his mother.

The hen was not
his mother.

So the baby bird went on.

"I have to find my mother!" he said. "But where? Where is she? Where could she be?"

Then he came to a
dog.

"Are you my mother?"
he said to the dog.

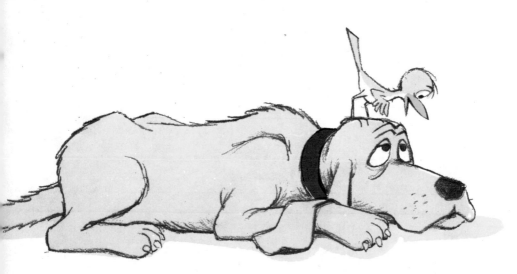

"I am not your mother.
I am a dog," said the dog.

The kitten was not
his mother.

The hen was not
his mother.

The dog was not
his mother.

So the baby bird went
on. Now he came to a
cow.

"Are you my mother?"
he said to the cow.

"How could I be your
mother?" said the cow. "I
am a cow."

The kitten and the hen
were not his mother.

The dog and the cow
were not his mother.

Did he have a mother?

"I did have a mother,"
said the baby bird. "I
know I did. I have to
find her. I will. I WILL!"

Now the baby bird did
not walk. He ran!

Then he saw a car.
Could that old thing be
his mother? No, it could not.

The baby bird did not
stop. He ran on and on.

Now he looked way,
way down. He saw a
boat. "There she is!" said
the baby bird.

He called to the boat,
but the boat did not
stop.

The boat went on.

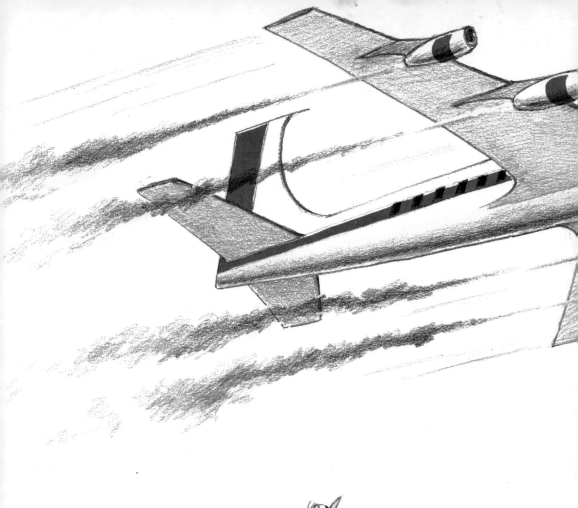

He looked way, way up.

He saw a big plane.

"Here I am, Mother,"

he called out.

But the plane did not
stop. The plane went on.

Just then, the baby bird
saw a big thing. This
must be his mother!

"There she is!" he said.
"There is my mother!"

He ran right up to it.
"Mother, Mother! Here
I am, Mother!" he said
to the big thing.

47

But the big thing just said, "Snort."

"Oh, you are not my mother," said the baby bird. "You are a Snort. I have to get out of here!"

49

But the baby bird could
not get away. The Snort
went up.

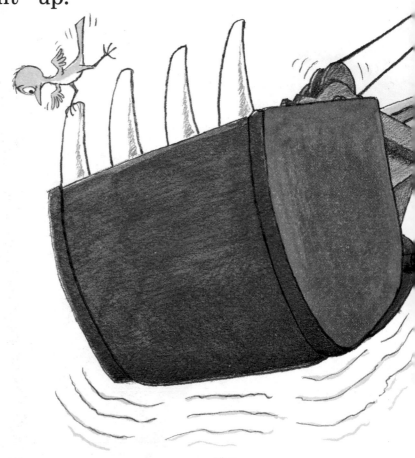

It went way, way up.
And up, up, up went
the baby bird.

But now, where was
the Snort going?

"Oh, oh, oh! What is
this Snort going to do to
me? Get me out of here!"

Just then, the Snort
came to a stop.

"Where am I?" said the
baby bird. "I want to go
home! I want my
mother!"

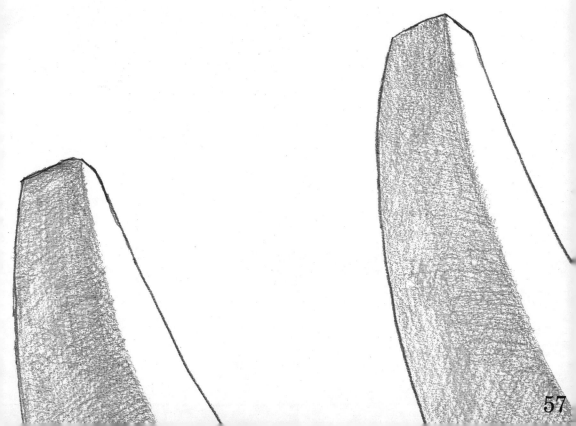

Then something
happened.

The Snort put that
baby bird right back in
the tree. The
baby bird was home!

Just then the mother
bird came back to the
tree. "Do you know who
I am?" she said to her
baby.

"Yes, I know who you
are," said the baby bird.

"You are not a kitten.

"You are not a hen.

"You are not a dog.

"You are not a cow.

"You are not a boat,
or a plane, or a Snort!"

"You are a bird, and
you are my mother."

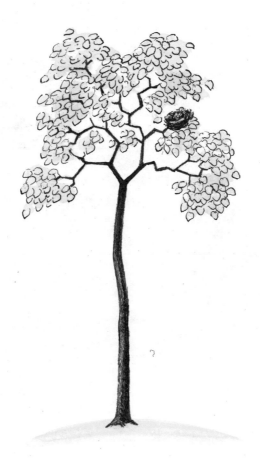